Part One

The bell rang throughout the trees, the broken branches and their rustic leaves. Through the meadows and the crops. Through the local towns brick homes and every inhabitants' ears. Ringing an unstoppable, sharp twang. Interrupting conversations between neighbours, and disturbing the children's play. Shattering every thought of every man and woman of the town.

Its third ring that year. That being significant as it rings only four times in a year, no more, no less. It came from the old abandoned church, that no one had come to claim after the priest's death five years before. So, it was left to dissolve into the earth and join the soil like the rest of humanity. However, since the priest's passing in 1800, the bell rang four times a year, each ring strategically placed. 12th February, 19th April, 4th October, and breaking the years cycle on November 26th. The bell rang on these days without fail.

The inhabitants of the town would use it as a ghost story to tell the children, "Go to bed and sleep well, or The Bell-ringer will come take you away". It seems strange that something that lives in such infamy can also live in such dark secrecy. As no one ever trekked the over grown dirt path to investigate the church. Apart from rowdy, hormone engulfed teens hoping to impress their friends with acts of bravery. But no one ever dared to enter the rotting doors, nor climb the spiralling stairs to the top of the tower. Maybe out of common sense, knowing nothing of worth would be up there. Or maybe out of fear. Fear that, like in classic stories, there would be an ugly, decrepit monster waiting to steal them away. How wrong they were.

The man in the tower was no monster, but was an incredibly tall, broad shouldered and muscular young man. He was not ugly or deformed, but beautiful, with striking blue eyes that sparkled in the moonlight. His head adorned with dark ebony locks, hanging jaggedly over his forehead. Light stubble clouded his face in an itchy mist, which he often unsuccessfully tried to shave with an old rusty blade. Large hands with nails closely trimmed, but his palms scared, fingertips course and bruised from years of ascending the church walls and handling the sharp iron bell. He had no twisted desires to kidnap a beautiful maiden, but was utterly content in his solitude.

He read expansive literature from the vast array of novels that he left piled in a leaning tower. He exercised regularly, climbing the church walls and the swinging among the rafters of his home. He ate well, being provided fruits and vegetables from the garden his father had made on the top of the church. He had lived in that church for over twenty-seven years, he had been born there, and had never left the stone slab walls that made his home.

He had never left for one reason. He was a bastard. A bastard boy of a priest and a prostitute. The priest had a wife, one which he loved dearly and truly, but unfortunately, even a man of strong a faith as he, couldn't resist The Bell-ringer's mother.

The Bell-ringer never saw a picture of his mother, but his father often spoke to him about her. He was told of her blonde hair which shined like gold in the sun. Blue eyes like that of the sapphire sea, able steal even the most weathered sailors' heart. How she often sung rhymes that could enchant anyone who heard the soft lull of her voice. His father sang one to him when he was just a young lad, and although it was his father's voice, it was his mother he heard sing.

"Dusk doth break through summer morn,
Two Lovers soft in silent bloom.
For Violet skies all faded worn,
Had cast away their winter moon."

"Your mother would sing that up here", his father told him, "She said that you would be able to hear her, and when you were born, you'd sing with her." His father told him, how he was the thing that brought joy to her otherwise depressing life. That him living was what she wanted. And that he shouldn't blame himself for her death.

See, his father was ashamed of what he had done, of his pregnant mistress and their unborn son. The Bell-ringers mother, so in love with the righteous priest, refused to be with any other man, and pleaded that they be together. Love blinding her to the disgust and shame that he felt towards her. So, when he begged and pleaded to her to stay in the church, to hide herself away, to wait to give birth, she accepted whole heartedly. Believing the lies that once the child was born, that they would run away together, and live in bliss. But life is cruel to those who are kind and good hearted. And as she laid bleeding out on the uncomfortable prickling wood. She saw the look on her lover's face as he held up a crying baby boy. Not one of anger, or shame. One of disappointment. Disappointed, that the baby had not died, like she soon would. Melancholy is what killed her in the end. The blood took her life. But melancholy took her soul. Her last act beckoning for her child, her boy, and naming him. Her words were lost on the Priests ears, and as he went to ask again, she died. The beautiful Margaret Smith, had died in a puddle of her own blood. In that moment the priest felt shame once more, but not towards his beautiful sleeping Margaret, or his crying boy. But himself.

He decided not to defile sweet Margaret's memory, or dishonour her more than he had done so already. He would not name the boy, as he was already named by Margaret. The Bell-ringer was born and baptised by blood on the 19th April, 1778.

The Bell-ringer lived in that same room where he had been born for his entire life. His father repented for his actions, and raised him like any other child, refusing to lie about the events that led to his birth. And The Bell-ringer grew up without hate or resentment in his heart. He loved his father. A man that as he saw it, was a close to God that a man could ever dream to reach. Honourable and kind, helpful to those in need of advice, always seeming to know right from wrong. Some of The Bell-ringer's favourite memories of his father was when weeping widows, lost men or just those seeking guidance came for advice. One time, when The Bell-ringer was 11 years old, he remembered climbing down onto the thin layer of weak wooden planks that barely separated him and the church goers. He heard a woman go up to his father in private and beg for God's forgiveness and his advice. She was pregnant out of wedlock. His fathers' words echo through The Bell-ringers mind most nights and days when he feels worthless.

"You need not God's forgiveness, only your own. Do not hate your child, as it is God's child as well as your own. Birth it, love it, and raise your child as if its father was the lord. For nothing is purer and more beautiful, than a loved child".

The woman thanked the priest, blessing him a long life, and walked with new found reassurance. The Bell-ringer clambered and searched for a slit or crack in the wood, risking the fall that would occur if too much weight was applied. He needed to see this woman's face. Into her eyes. For to him, she was his mother, and he her son. But just as he found a break in the wooden planks, all he saw was her dress slink slowly out of his life. That woman never came back to church again. And The Bell-ringer's mind often wondered what happened to her and her baby. Wondering if her child was destined the same fate as him, or if it the mother and child could run free in sunlit meadows in view of the world. That is why he didn't hate his father, because his father loved him, but had to keep up reputation and his life. The Bell-ringer understood it, as the sheep understands its destiny for the slaughter, content with knowing he would live and die in that church.

The Bell-ringer was not alone however, at least not in his mind. He had his mother, her grave lay in the garden, guarded from public sight by the edges of the roof tiles. He would always tend to the flowers that sprouted from the earth around her. His father had told him how the world feeds itself, how God never takes life, but passes it on to the next creature, and in his mother's place grave grew passionate red roses that bloomed seductively each year. The Bell-ringer believed they bloomed to celebrate his mothers' birthday, the 4th of October. As the petals were at their most fiery around this time, and soon afterwards, would crinkle, wither, die, and fall gracefully back into the soil. And on her birthday, he would talk to her all day about what he had done, what he had read, what he'd seen of the forest and its many creatures. Often, he would sing the rhyme he could never forget to her, with tears in his eyes and a croak in his throat.

5

His father would comfort him on his mother's birthday. Never interrupting however, allowing his son to let his tears flow and water his mother's remains. But when his son meekly came back into the tower, he was met by a hug and professions of love, then they would celebrate with cake, and would bless his mother's memory. The Bell-ringer loved his father. And it is easy to see, that The Bell-ringers downfall began on the 26th November, 1800.

The priest had not been to the church for over a week, not even for his Sunday Sermon. The last time they spoke, his father's voice rasped from his parched lips, his drooping eyelids barely able to lift themselves up. Stumbling out of the church, promising his son a quick return as soon as he was able, with no hug or kiss. Simply hobbling away.

Then after weeks of pining after his father, he heard people entering the church, assuming that his father had recovered from his illness, he made his way down through the rafters to watch his father preach. He thought of how he would tell his father how he missed him dearly, how he loved him, that next time his father is ill that he will take care of him. He was so enthusiastic and hopeful that he remained smiling even after he saw the priest who spoke was not his father. So, he lay delicately on the paper-thin boards, and listened to the mumblings of the priest.

"Great man... Fredrick Conra... missed...". It was a funeral. His father's name gnawed at his ears. The Bell-ringer let his breath slowly seep like poison into the church below. The roof moaned in pain under the weight of The Bell-ringer's loss. He couldn't move. Paralysed with fear of his reality.

He heard the church goers sing their hymns and say their goodbyes, but The Bell-ringer's eyes were blinded and his ears deafened. As they left the church to go bury his father, he saw his step mother, and his half-sister being consoled by the sorrowful guests. His sister, no older than 10, who, behind the red puffy eyes and lips which quivered from the November chill, looked familiar to him. Not only did she have his father's hazel eyes, but also the same nose, slightly pointing at the tip. But this new-found kinship felt empty. A pit in his soul grew when his father died. A pit because he never got to say goodbye. Never got to tell his father not to be afraid, that'll he'll stay hidden because his love would outlive both of them. He never got to feel his father arms round his. Never would hear him tell him stories of far off lands, or strong heroes valiantly saving fair maidens. He loved his father, and he couldn't be by his graveside. And that was the first spark of hate which burnt his heart.

When he saw the priest give his father his last rights, the priest asked the family of his father to be the first to throw the soil. He wanted to go down. Reveal himself. Be with his father. But he couldn't. Instead he went to the rusty iron bell that hung silently dormant as it had for years, and grasped it either side, forcing his arms out as wide as they would go. He felt his muscles begin to stretch and twist by the sheer mass of the bell, his hands slicing against the edge. Allowing his sadness to become anger, his cries became yells as he pulled the old bell towards him and pushing it back out with monstrous strength. The pull did nothing to the ancient bell, its rusty chains convulsing like a serpent suffocating its prey. Blood already swelled in his fists, and sweat fell on his brow. He pulled again. The chains holding the bell groaning as The Bell-ringers muscles did. The Bell-ringer did this over and over. Until the bell sang its deathly tune.

The bell pierced his ears with a fury he had never felt before. His brain exploded with each strike. His screams melted in with the rings. He revelled in it, the pain was euphoric, it taught him what his life meant. It meant pain, to respect those who had created his existence. And as his father's wife looked up to the tower hearing the eruptions, she smiled. Smiling as she believed the priest had out of respect asked someone to ring it. Smiling at each chime, as she thought of the great honourable man that her husband was.

The church goers soon left, and The Bell-ringers pain subsided, as he staggered out into the night, face streaked with tears and hands torn apart. Smothered in liquid crimson, he fell upon his mother's flowery tomb, blood weeping onto the roses.

"Father says, that you're, you're in heaven even though you sinned b-because God forgives everyone if their good at heart. He told me, about Mary Madeline, she was Jesuses friend, he loved her and, and she was a prostitute. So, so I know you're up there waiting for me. And so is father, so maybe you two may meet again... I'm not sure, but I think he missed you almost as much as I do." He wiped tears from his eyes and cleared his voice, trying to regain control of his ragged and disproportion breaths. "I really wish you wasn't up there though. Because. I'm alone now. And I know I have to be. For both of you, I need to protect both of you. And I will. I promise I will. I swear, I'll die before anyone finds out about me. So then when I do, I can see you. And you can hug and kiss me, and you can sing to me. I really want you to sing to me. Plea-please." Tears clawed out of his eyes.

He stood, sucking in the piercing frosted air through pursed lips, ascending onto the roofs peak to look at his father's grave. Surrounded by flowers, charms and ornaments. He whispered to himself his promise, "I will not abandon you father".

The Bell-ringer went to turn when he saw a pair of amber eyes looking at him from the shadow of the forest. A lonely beast, not knowing its purpose, nor meaning of its existence. Like all man-kind, blind to the impact and mark they will make on the world, without the choice to change what their actions mean for the future of humanity. But The Bell-ringer knew his meaning, his purpose. He will stay and wait. Wait till the day his flesh, blood and bone naturally feed the soil, his voice unheard, his face unseen, his life unknown. His effect on the world will be that he left no mark, dent or scratch. As if he never had existed at all.

For five years he rang that bell, undisturbed by the people of the nearby town, who only occasionally turned up to abandon flowers on half-forgotten graves. His half-sister came up most Sunday's to their shared father's grave, he saw her age and mature into a wonderfully beautiful person. She was the only family he had, and he wished she would come be in the tower with him. But he knew his place, to stay hidden. That was until October 4th in 1805. When the past came knocking.

Part Two

The Bell-ringer laid in complete darkness, no light of the moon or stars being powerful enough to break through the iron bell that hung protectively over him. Pure silence apart from the muffled echo of each breath he took, laying in a puddle of blood that leaked from the reopened scars on his palms. His mind was exhausted and dizzy from the pain, his mind slipping in and out a consciousness. But his hazy head was roused by a creak of the boards leading up to his home. Slowly but surely, he heard weight being shifted, step to step. The Bell-ringer slinked out from beneath his bell on all fours, spreading out his weight as his blood limped out leaving red prints in his wake.

The door creaked cautiously open, crinkling at the hinges, revealing a cackling flame protruding through searchingly. The beacon swayed side to side, and once it concluded that nothing living was in the room it delved in deeper, pulling the intruder behind. The Bell-ringer was among the rafters, slowly and delicately swinging silently, fearing the light that the little flame radiated. The intruder searched among The Bell-ringers few belongings, inspecting his clothes, peering into the books that lay strewn across the floor boards and finally setting his eyes on the garden beyond. The Bell-ringer's breath quickened and nostrils flared with fear, no longer able to follow the man from the safety of the darkness. So as the man entered the colourful cemetery, The Bell-ringer hung and dropped ominously behind him, falling to all fours and slipping into the slick vegetation.

The intruder continued to search and The Bell-ringer watched with piercing eyes, as the man looked bewilderingly at the grave. The light cast a luminous glow over the garden, and The Bell-ringers blue eyes flared with an amber glare which burned into the intruder's heart. Bending to one knee, the intruder reached out with a hand caressing the crimson petals as he looked at the name etched perfectly onto the stone tablet.

The Bell-ringer felt his blood thump in his skull, hearing each beat of his heart ringing in his ears like the bell's painful shrieks. Not out of fear, but out of rage. How someone could enter his home. Could go to his mother's grave. How someone would dare defile the natural order of his mother's essence. And as he saw the man fingertips tighten on the thorny stem, about to pluck his mother away from him, The Bell-ringer snapped. The beast slowly crept from the woods one paw at a time.

Throwing himself forward like a lion leaping upon unwitting prey roaring as he did so. But the intruder, caught off guard, swung around widely, and the brass lamp connected with the corner of The Bell-ringers eye, dropping him quickly to the floor. As the Bell-ringer went to push himself back up, the brass lamp swiftly struck down on his spine sprawling him out on the soil as he meekly stared at his mother's grave. The rose still intact.

"Who the fuck are ya", The man growled at The Bell-ringer, crushing his wounded back with the sole of his boot. "What the fuck did you do too her, ya fucking bastard".

"Leave... The rose". The Bell-ringer wheezed, he cared not for what would happen to him, but his mother's roses mustn't be disturbed.

The man looked at the roses that flourished upon grave, and relinquishing his foot off The Bell-ringers back, grabbed him by the scruff of his hair, pulling his head up to meet his eyes.

"Who is this woman to you?" His eyes blazed with a rage The Bell-ringer had never witnessed before, but he saw the eyes looked desperately at his own for answers. The eyes were blue like his, but cold and icy with age. Wrinkles had secured themselves across the man's face but still held a hint of youth.

Through bloodied teeth and a numb jaw, The Bell-ringer replied, "My mother", suddenly feeling the same fury that he had felt the day of his father's funeral. The fury that, until this moment, he had never told anyone that, and it felt so good to tell someone.

Suddenly dropping his head, the man staggered backwards, sitting exhausted on a mound of dirt, staring at The Bell-ringer slowly pushing himself up.

"Jesus fucking Christ. That bastard actually put her up here", he looked disgustedly at his surroundings, his eyes settling on the make shift grave that lay shoddily among the manufactured garden. "And he fucking left her here", a sob rose in his throat, "that bastard stole her away."

"Who?", The Bell-ringer weakly replied.

"That fucking priest. No one believed me but I knew it. I knew he put her somewhere. So, no one would know his shame." He spat the words out like venom. He then really saw The Bell-ringer, his nephew, his sister's son. "You've always been up here ain't ya?"

The Bell-ringer only looked at him fearfully. The boiling rage had simmered, and now all he could think about was what he had done. This man knew he existed.

"The priest forced Maddy up here", he nodded at The Bell-ringer's bloated face. "My sister. I'm, I'm John…"

John kept talking about how he had left after Maddy disappeared when he was young, but always knew the priest stole her away. That he had heard of the strange little church, that the priest had died, and so decided to return to find Maddy. But The Bell-ringer payed no attention to his uncles' story, instead focused on one thing, "the priest forced Maddy up here". It rung in his mind, awakening him to an idea that had never occurred to him before. That his mother and father both didn't want him. That he was the consequence unhappiness.

"My father didn't force her". He whispered, almost inaudibly. "She loved him. They were gonna have me and then leave. She loved me". He said defiantly, angry that this stranger made him doubt his beautiful mother, who sang and cared for him in the tower.

"No, she didn't", John now stared just as angrily back at The Bell-ringer with the same fury in his eyes. "He forced her away, he would have kept you both locked up here if he had the chance", he stared back at the grave, "If he had had the chance".

The Bell-ringer realised he had to do something. John would tell people about his mother, about his father, about him. It would mean that his mother's death, his father's guilt and his own 27 years of solitude was all for nothing. A man will do anything to protect and defend the life he has lived. Even if their lives were full of suffering and pain, they want a justification, a purpose behind it. Because if it all amounted to nothing, then what was the point of it. And it's amazing how quickly one can turn to the darkness within them, when before their purity was blinding.

The Bell-ringer stood towering over John, who now seemed insignificant on the floor, his bulky chest leaning down towards ground gorilla like, expanding his already impressive frame. His face throbbed from the bronze lamp on the right side, his eye seemingly grown out past its normal place, and the top of his lip was swelled out of recognition. He was truly beast like.

"You can't leave", he said calmly and coldly, even though deep down he was afraid of what he was going to do. However, it was nothing to the fear John now felt, with a lumbering giant looming over him, he realised the danger he was in.

"Come with me", he said as he started to slip away and stand. "Come with me, we'll go to the village and explain".

"No one can know I'm here", The Bell-ringer said factually, stalking John as he started to walk backwards to make his escape.

"I won't tell anyone".

"… Yes, you will". The Bell-ringer looked sadly into John's eyes, hoping John saw the humanity in him, hoping he understood why he had to do this. But John saw only a monster. A disgusting creature living in the bell tower. A monster that killed his sister.

He turned and ran, he was fast, but even with The Bell-ringers half-crippled spine he was still faster. And just as John got to the door of the stairs, rough gravelly hands clasped round his neck. The Bell-ringer's hand securely fastened and lifted John from the ground with ape like strength, staring tearfully into his uncle's fearful eyes.

"She- Hates- You". The last spiteful words of a man who knows he is doomed.

The Bell-ringer, in an act of animalistic aggression, smashed his uncle's skull against the cruel bell. Making not a piecing howl, but a sickly thud. And as he crushed his uncle's skull, over and over and over again, the thuds got weaker and weaker, until there was barely a sound.

John was left lifeless floating in a river of red. The Bell-ringer knew not what to do. His mind was still spiralling sporadically. His eyes kept being dragged back to John's face. Or the smashed skull that remained. His nose seemed to of sunk back into his face. His mouth had no clear distinction in where it was originally as it now gaped open in an unnatural look of surprise. His eye sockets seemed to of closed in on themselves, blinding him to the disgusting mash of bone and tissue that his face had become.

The Bell-ringer left his lifeless corpse slumped on the bell, and had secluded himself to his mother's grave. He knelt, staring emotionless at his mother's name.

"I did a bad thing mother. I'm sorry... I hurt your brother... I'm sure you loved him and that he loved you. Bu- At least... your together now." A pleasant realisation entered his mind, "You two can see each other again, and be happy, and laugh, and play, and then he'll of forgiven me and understand why by the time I see you all!" His smile quickly faded into a grimace.

"What if, I don't see you again. Father said that as long as you're not cruel at heart God forgives. That's why he's forgiven... Did he force you up here? He put you up here because of me. Forced you up here. And you died cause of him and me. We murdered you..."

He stared solemnly at his mother's name. All it represented was love and hope for him, that she had given him life out of love. Now it was tainted and corrupted by John. She had birthed him and died full of hate and bitterness. And the beast crawled further out the forest, lurking in the pit.

"Everything has a place in this world", The Bell-ringer's fathers voice echoed in his mind as he remembered them gardening together. His father put up a tank to collect rain water, so the Bell-ringer had clean water to drink, a compost pile to use as fertiliser where he should put dead leaves and excrement in to feed the crops. Self-sustainable. So that he would never have to leave.

"Death feeds life" the Bell-ringer whispered slowly and softly.

He hacked and clawed at his uncle's limbs, tendrils of veins slipping out of the joints as the flesh was crudely torn apart, leaving flaps of skin still connected to the lifeless corpse. He tore till only his uncle's torso and mangled head remained, and the rest. The rest he fed to the beast.

The mourning dawn rose softly over the church, its molten rays bathing The Bell-ringer in a light pink hew. The Bell-ringer's eyes consumed the light eagerly having spent an eternity staring into the abyss of the night sky. Thousands of beautifully bright stars seemed dead and meaningless to his eyes, the mechanical outline of solar systems and constellations. Never moving or changing, seemed so against the natural order of the universe. The Bell-ringer pondered what will happen to them when they die. Whether they will softly fizzle into oblivion and be consumed by nothingness, or maybe in a glorious explosion that would ignite the universe in a beautiful expansive shine. A thought grew in his mind, if the stars he saw glaring in darkness were already dead, if before they were silent and forgotten, but it was death that gave them their beauty. Like they never even existed at all.

The warmth rushed over his body and he let out a slow heave of relief. Relief that the sun still rose over him, that in reality, nothing had changed.

He went to the tub of cool crisp water that had been filled peacefully the day before by a comforting shower, and proceeded to clean the dried blood that came off in red flakes. He massaged his still throbbing half closed eye, and flicked the blood off of his mouth. He stalked over to a mirror that hung on the outside of the wall separating him and the corpse. And stared numbly at his reflection.

His right eye had been swallowed by swelling flesh, and the right side of his top lip hung over his bottom lazily. Not only this but the scars on his hand were reopened after ringing the bell the night before. The clotted blood would not hold back the waves of blood for much longer as he performs his daily routine, and so he knew he had to get his rags that lay among the corpse.

He slunk nervously into his room, disturbed by how untouched it looked, everything exactly where he had left it apart from a few books picked up and dropped. Even the blood that seeped from the corpse was not unusual, the floorboards had always been stained by blood; his mothers and then his. But the corpse. The corpse was different. Motionless and stoic, yet The Bell-ringer felt the anger inside its veins as it lay crumpled on the bell on which it was murdered. The stench was by far worse on The bell-ringer's senses than its appearance. The torn and already decaying flesh, the stench of excrement was revolting, filling up the room with a musk of moist and heavy air.

The Bell-ringer gingerly crept towards the bell, refusing his one good eye from staring at the mutilated body, holding his breath as he did so. But even as he held his breath, he felt the stench linger in the back of his throat, and he vomited next to the body, adding to the aura of death.

He quickly darted back outside as soon as his hands connected with his bloodied rags, peering accusingly at the corpse, searching for a sign it had moved. Of course, his uncle had not fallen or slipped an inch, not changed at all. Unnatural.

That day The Bell-ringer cleaned the room. Dry heaving as he pulled his uncle out, and continuing to do so as he scrubbed the floors of his sin. The corpse he was unsure what to do with, the beast of the forest would not want to eat rotting meat. So, he chopped it up with more care and respect than the night previously, and placed it in the compost so that it may feed the soil. All except the skull, which he flayed and cleaned, placing it on the corner of a shelf in his room, as a sign of respect to his uncle's memory. He took his uncles clothes and all his belongings; a pipe, matches, pocket watch, a few pennies, oil for his lamp, fresh tobacco and a pocket knife. He inspected all these things with the curiosity of an infant.

"Smoking is the habit of men without God", his father told him when men after church would go outside and smoke their pipes, the scent of tobacco would surround and conquer the church. "They say it relieves them of their troubles and ailments, argh!" he threw his arms up emphatically. "God, my son, God puts men through turmoil to test them! To see if you trust and believe in him to show you the way out. Promise me, my son, never give in to mans primal urge to seek the easy resolution."

He believed his father, even when he saw in his jacket pocket a pipe of his own. He never doubted the validity and truth behind his father's words. Although, he also remembered the kids that would run up to the church and hide among the trees, and in acts of rebellion, smoke from their fathers stolen pipes. How they would cough and heave with agony after each intake. Maybe that was why his father made him swear to never smoke, for fear he would draw attention from passers-by with his coughing. His father lied just to hide him away. Refused him something that could made any man happy, that was worth going through fits of coughing for.

He put the pipe to his lips, lit a match and breathed in the poisonous fumes. He consumed the smoke feverously, causing him to cough and wretch, the flavour soaking into his throat and rotting his teeth. But the smell and taste of the dirtied corpse was gone. His mind was fuzzy, and legs quivered and he continued to smoke the pipe like it was the greatest thing he had ever had in his life. It hurt his throat, but he didn't mind, he preferred it to the taste of death lurking within.

Realising the cathartic nature of the pipe, he went into his room, burrowing himself under his bell. Letting the fumes surround and play joyfully inside, the light seeping in from the rims giving the smoke form and life. Hot, sweet stench of tobacco washed over him, and his mind slowly faded into blackness.

He awoke an hour or so later, cleansed and pure. He slipped out the bottom of his bell, and went to lift up the bell to allow the smoke to escape the prison it remained in. It was harder than before however, his lungs were weak, he was barely able to walk, but still he prevailed. As he pulled the bell up and felt his legs sway and beg to collapse, he fixed them harder into the wood. The smoke poured out and swam around the room like ghosts. The Bell-ringer watched as the phantoms slipped into his uncle's skull, flowing in and out of the broken sockets and jaw serpent like.

He tried to continue on as he had done before, paying no mind to what he had done. But while he tried to forget, the town grew more suspicious. A man had disappeared without a trace when going up to the church. Stories grew wild of how The Bell-ringer could turn people into the wind and trees, that he grows stronger and soon would leave his home to wreak havoc on the town. Children believed in the beast, while the adults tried to pay no mind. They knew something ominous was in that forest, and they knew one day they would have to face up to it. But they didn't want to face their dark reality, simply waiting for it to fade from their thoughts.

But nothing can stay in hidden forever.

Part Three

Darkness enveloped the world earlier and earlier as winter brought in iced winds and frozen air. Winter's were hard for The Bell-ringer, the cold always managing to find cracks in the stone and scrape its way into his room, scratching at his skin with frosted claws. His crops would wither, the soil turn baron and unnourishing. But the night brought him freedom, and he would pay the chill no mind as he climbed the slippery tower, to sit upon the spire and stare out enviously at the world he was refused.

He looked out to the town, ablaze with the beauty of a thousand burning candles, the air warm with songs that The Bell-ringer smiled and clapped along to. The 31st of October, Halloween, when the ghosts of the dead would revisit the living. Having his home be next to a grave yard as a wildly imaginative youth, he would imagine skeletons and ghouls escaping their frozen tombs. But his father had always calmed his fears.

"The soul doesn't remain on the Earth my son. God accepts good souls in open arms, and every man and woman in this cemetery were good people. Believe in me."

What if his father had lied? What if they all had their own beasts that hid in the pit of their souls. His father had stolen away his mother. He himself had killed his uncle. How could either man be considered good? Or maybe, if every soul is cruel, its not cruel to kill. Maybe his uncle John was far worse than him, and so it was just to kill him.

But his mother was not a cruel soul. She didn't deserve what happened to her. What his father had done. The Bell-ringers mind was dampened by a thought that none of the burning celebrations could warm; what if his father awoke tonight.

"Come on, mind the hole there!", a deep voice commanded.

The Bell-ringer was so shaken by the out-cries he almost lost his balance, but he gripped on tightly to the spire as his legs licked the towers edge limply. He hunted the trees for the voice, until he saw three lonely lights setting the forest aflame.

"This is horrible", another man laughed, "My god, if I fall I'm going to kill you".

"Don't be so dramatic", a woman's voice. The Bell-ringer's sister's, distinct as she always put emphasis of the first syllable of each word, recognising it from Sunday's where she would come sit with their father.

"Scared of falling? And you wanted to go fight, ha!", the deep voiced man stifled a chuckle.

"I'm scared of whatever is in these fucking woods if I'm gonna be honest with you", he replied, nervously chuckling.

"Oh no, The Bell-ringer! He'll swoop down and steal you away", his sister said in fake hysterics. "He'd be the first person to show you any interest."

The Bell-ringer listened and smiled, but wondered what they meant by "The Bell-ringer".

"Is that what they call me?", he thought, "The Bell-ringer". His thoughts were cut off by hearing them wander innocently out of the tree line and into his domain. The light blinding the bell-ringer's eyes to their faces as they pulled open the rotting oak door. The Bell-ringer's eyes widened with curiosity and fear, as the group of rebellious misfits hurriedly escaped into the church.

While no one had come up to his room before his uncle had, people had entered into the church before. All he had to do was hide away, tucked between the space separating his room and the hall, and discreetly watch. He descended carefully down the tower, making sure not lose his grasp on the ice laden stone. Gently placing himself down in his garden and swiftly entering his home to slip beneath the floor boards.

The group crept slowly into the church, their childhood fears of monsters and ghouls surrounding them in a frosty embrace. The three lights departed one another, destroying the peaceful darkness that the church lived in. Speaking in hushed tones as if not to wake a sleeping beast, they stalked curiously inspecting the cluttered mess of unwanted items that called the church their home. One of the men looked cautiously at the door that led to The Bell-ringers lair, fixating on it as if he could feel the evil that oozed from within. He made his way slowly over to it, the other man and The Bell-ringer's sister noticed and followed loyally behind.

The Bell-ringer quickly shot up into the groaning wood, scurrying back to stare worriedly at his unopened door, listening to the wooden stairs creak. He knew he could not hide as he did before, and he had no intention of hurting anyone. He needed to act.

Prowling over to the door, careful not to make a sound, he opened it ever so slightly, and let his breath grow hot and rugged at the back of his throat; he growled. He got on all floors and scratched at the wood to imitate the sound of unkept paws. He growled louder until he started barking like a mad dog. When he heard the hesitation of footsteps, he knew they were afraid. Roaring, he charged down the stairs on all floors, letting his weight crash down on the shaking wooden frames, his body plummeting and hurtling into walls as he did so.

The group turned and threw themselves back down to the safety of the wide-open hall, too afraid to meet whatever animal had made the tower its home. They ran and didn't look back till they were on the other side of the crumbling oak doors, slamming it shut to trap the beast. The Bell-ringer's sister only saw one thing in the quickly closing darkness. Her light shining upon a pair of amber eyes.

The Bell-ringer looked longingly at the shut doors, wiping spittle from his lips, he felt his eyes grow heavy with tears. Tears because of how terribly lonely he was. He slowly lumbered back up to his room, and sat among his mother's flowers, playing with the feeble petals that slowly peeled from the stem. It would be dead soon; the flowers will wither and he'll be without a mother again until they bloom again in the new year. But until then, he only had his uncle for company, and The Bell-ringer felt his uncles empty sockets burn into his soul unforgivingly.

He watched as the lamps swayed and rocked on the foggy green. Dancing peacefully between the dense darkness until one slowly peeled away and seeped back into the night. The other two seemed to halt their waltz and crash violently, like two stars melting into each other. Until, without any warning they were extinguished just behind the tree line.

Muffled shrieks and gasps crept out of the old woods. The Bell-ringer leaned slightly over the edge of the roof to see, but not even his nocturnal eyes couldn't distinguish any shape or form separate from the trees. Instead, cocking his head to one side, focusing his hearing to ignore the howls of the wind. The gasps grew louder, until he heard his sister shout defiantly, yet with ripe with fear.

"Get off of me!".

"Shut it!", The deep voiced man commanded.

The Bell-ringer saw a mixture of outlines just behind layers of protective brambles. He listened to his sister scream through muzzled lips. He heard the rip of her dress. The pounds of her hands against her attacker's chest

The Bell-ringer's fingers clamped round the tiles of the roof, as he stared pathetically at the ground refusing to look at the violation of his sister.

He couldn't leave his home. He couldn't help her. He had never left his home, he couldn't. Then he heard the tree shake with a brutal sting. His sister's muffled screams were non-existent, but they echoed in The Bell-ringer's head. The silence over-whelming him. He felt the old stone crack under his palms. His grip loosening as he lifted himself up, and flung himself cascading down the church walls, flittering to the cool slick grass with the grace of gliding feather.

The grass was cold and wet beneath The Bell-ringer's bare feet, the water letting his feet slide on the soil as he leapt and bound to his sister's aid. The glare of a thousand eyes watched. The owls halted their hooting. The Foxes paralysed in their lairs. The beast of the forest watching with eager glee. The Bell-ringer was free.

Baring his teeth in a grim smile. His eyes grew mad with animalistic pleasure. He was overwhelmed by feverous excitement; he was free from his cage. His emotions bubbled in his heart, his fiery hatred setting his blood ablaze, melting the chains that had formed around his mind. Forging into a ravenous desire to inflict himself on the world that knew nothing of his existence.

Brambles and thorns protected the violator who lay upon his sister, her dress crudely torn leaving her breasts bare to the cruel cold temperatures. The man heard the brambles and twigs shatter, and the earth quiver under the stampeding weight of The Bell-ringer. And as he turned to witness the behemoth charging at him, he shot up in fright and cowered backwards. He opened his mouth to either make a desperate apology, explanation, or a threat. He was denied the privilege of professing any.

The Bell-ringer wasted no time searching for the humanity in this man, seeing his half pulled up trousers as proof of his wickedness. The Bell-ringer gripped the man by the throat as he laid petrified, and lifted the sinner to meet his raging eyes. The man rattled and gasped, trying to pronounce his final words. But The Bell-ringer would not allow him to poison his mind as his uncle had. Instead closing his hand to a fist around the man's neck, letting the bone crack and the windpipe squelch.

The corpse crumpled into the dirt, folding in on itself as his bones collapsed. The corpse looked at The Bell-ringer with surprise and acceptance etched on it, not the look of fear The Bell-ringer expected, nor the anger he had hoped for. It wasn't like John. John's face was wiped from his head, it was easy to forget he was human. But here he saw a man. A man about to commit a terrible sin, one of the worst ones his father told him, but still. A man, with a mother and father. A man whose last memory, was the swollen face of a monster.

He looked at his sister apologetically, defeated by his impulsive rage, studying her petite head, which pulsed with blood from where it had been thrown into the tree. How vulnerable she was, clothes torn as if ravaged by a pack of wolves. She was so beautiful.

The Bell-ringer looked back spitefully at the corpses face, and the pity he felt vanished. He saw this man for what he was, while he had no glimmering eyes, profuse fur or deadly claw. He saw the beast within. Defeated and whimpering, but a beast none the less. And with contempt at the weakness of the beast for going after such innocent prey, he stamped hard and true, sending the nose receding back into the skull. And he wondered, if the beast in this man, was the same as his father's.

His sister stirred with a whimper and a quick exhale of precious warmth. There was no time, she could not be left open to the brutality of men, beasts and nature all alike. So, with a refined sense of duty, he plucked the edges of her dress, folding them over each other, and lifted her up with gentle ease. She had to go to the tower. He must return back to his prison.

Carrying his sister on his mighty shoulders he mounted the church walls and climbed with more haste then sense. Constantly feeling his fingers slip, but he refused to fall, tearing into the hard ice and continuing his ascent. Only slowing down once his feet touched the unmoving soil of his garden, moving as swiftly as the wind to his bell. Placing his sister carefully beneath, shielding her from the evil world he had saved her from.

"You shouldn't have done that", John's skull smugly mumbled through his stationary jaw.

"What was I mean to do", The Bell-ringer pleaded, "I couldn't let him, let him do what he was... I couldn't. Father would have wanted me to protect her."

"The priest. The bastard who stole my sister away and let her die. Who kept you up here, his own son. You think he loved you boy? He wanted you to die with Maddy. You think he would care what happened to her?"

"Yes. Of course, he would, he always said, what that man was going to do, was the worst sin." The Bell-ringer said defiantly.

"Just like smoking tobacco? Just like disobeying those who loved him? He was a liar, he lied to hide you away. He raped Ma- "

The skull was silenced by the fist The Bell-ringer smashing through the floor boards.

"That. Is. Enough…"

"Are you scared nephew? That your lonely, pathetic life, has been to protect that kind of man?"

The Bell-ringer made no reply, only slowly dragging his fist from the wood, splinters painfully embedded themselves into his knuckles.

"…What about her?"

"I'm not sure", The Bell-ringer couldn't meet the skulls empty sockets, instead looking exhaustedly at the ground.

"They'll come looking for him. When they find him, they'll search up here… You gonna wring her neck like you did him?"

"No!"

"How about smash her face into the bell like you did me?"

"No!"

"Why not?", the skull grew angrier and louder, "You to good for that? To holy? You're a monster, 'The Bell-ringer', ugh."

The Bell-ringer's eyes widened and forehead relaxed at a realisation. 'The Bell-ringer'. They called him-

"uhhhh… wha…", The Bell-ringer's sister awoke with a quiet groan, echoing in the void of the empty bell. "Whe- where, where am I?", she started hitting the bell docilely, the only audible thing being her worried tear-filled gasps.

The Bell-ringer froze. Should he hide? Let her find her own way out? Or should he help? A brilliantly naïve thought entered his mind, "she'll stay with me".

He lifted up the bell, revealing the overly distressed damsel, whom upon one glance at her protector let out a scream.

He was by far the largest man she had ever encountered, with a grey under shirt that stretched securely round his chest and arms and ripped at the collar. Trousers which were far to short, tightly hugging half way down his calf. His bare feet covered in dirty moisture, a red right hand, and clear facial damage. However, even with the swollen eye, she saw a distinctly attractive young man. And while she was still fearful of what this stranger could do to her, she was comforted by those sapphire eyes.

"Where am I?", she said cautiously, crawling out of the bell on the far side of her brother, never breaking eye contact. Her question was only met with silence and a scared look in her saviours' eyes.

"I said, where am I?", she repeated with more fire in her voice, trying her hardest to fight away the tremble in her throat.

The Bell-ringer opened his mouth to reply, but stopped himself, gulping visibly and lowering the bell.

"What the fuck is going on", this time she could not hold back the tears, as she sobbed into her palms. The Bell-ringer paced slowly over to his sister, and as she looked up at him, he dropped to his knees, and unwrapped the bandage around his nearly healed scars.

"I'm sorry." He wiped her eyes away with the rag, smearing blood under her eyes.

"That man tried to hurt you... He didn't, don't worry..." he stared into his sisters' eyes, and truly admired his sister's beauty.

"Who are you? Where am I?", she said through teary eyes.

"The church. Well the tower, the tower of the church." The Bell-ringer stuttered his words, his tongue seemingly becoming useless in his mouth.

"Why?", her jaw lax and eyes squinting trying to make sense of the stranger. "Why, here?"

"I uh... this is where I live." He looked round suddenly embarrassed by the way in which he dwelled, which he assumed was primitive compared to the no doubt glorious abode his sister lived in.

"What, why?", she suddenly looking concerned, jaw tightening and those brown eyes widening. "Was you in here earlier, was you the- ". She looked around nervously, grasping at her wounded head trying to make sense of everything. Trying to make sense of whether she should fear this stranger.

"No, no, no, well. Well yes. But", desperation fled into The Bell-ringer's voice. "I had to keep you away, otherwise you would of seen me. And, and you can't see me."

"Why? How long have you been here?".

The Bell-ringer looked into his sisters' eyes, the eyes of his kin. He felt in love.

"I've been here since I was born, 27 years ago..." A smile curled round the sides of his lips. "Our father wanted me to stay hidden. I think he would allowed me to help you..."

They stared at each other for a small eternity. Her mouth jutted, as if to say something, anything to break the perpetual cycle of silence she felt trapped in. But she couldn't utter a single word. She just looked at her brothers face, and while she felt like she should object and accuse the loiterer of lying, she already knew he was being honest.

It all made sense, her fathers' constant absence, spending hour upon hour alone (thought to be alone at least) in the church. How he would take whole meals, treats and cakes up to the tower and appear empty handed that same night. And she saw the high cheek bones of her father, with the same hesitant smile he always had on her brothers face.

"The day he died, he left our house. Pushed away the doctors, me and my mother both. We screamed at him to come back to bed but he refused. As soon as he heard us ask for a priest... He got quite far, all the way up to the edge of the forest. He said... He wanted to say goodbye. He kept saying that, he wanted to say goodbye and we was all so, confused. He fell and started crying. Begging God to forgive him.", she wiped a tear from her eye. "When I bent down to ask him why, he pointed to the church, pushing my chin upwards to see the tower rising over the tree tops... He died looking at where he was pointing." She looked sadly at her brother, whose smile tightened and eyes quivered with a tear.

"He... He must have wanted to make sure I wouldn't tell anyone. That I'd stay hidden, he shouldn't have worried". The Bell-ringer said with a shaky voice, that in his last moments his father did care, that The Bell-ringer had done what his father had wanted.

His sister looked at him with sad realisation, that her brother was imprisoned by their father, and brainwashed to accept his fate as a necessary evil. But she saw the innocence in him, the childlike desire to please those he loves.

"No. No I think he meant to bring you back. He felt bad... Come back with me, we'll look after you.", she requested firmly, her smooth voice soothing extinguishing the glowing cinders that laid in his heart.

"No."

"Why?"

"This is where he wanted me. I need to stay here. For both of them".

"Listen to me", her voice heated up, "he didn't want you here, come back with me, we'll go now".

"You can't go." His words stunned even him. His realisation she would tell just as John would have done. And she started to feel the same fear John felt as the monster of the tower stood over her.

"Listen to me its ok."

"No, no, stay with me", desperation blurted itself into his voice as he dropped to his knees. "Out there is dangerous and cruel. What happened to my mother. What that man almost did to you. I can keep you safe, we can be happy." He almost believed she would accept. That she would drop her connection to the world and succumb to the simple, confined life that even he had begun to detest. But he truly, naïvely believed, that maybe his solitude would end.

"Wait… What did you… What happened to Walter?", her distress grew when even after she repeated her question, she was greeted by guilty silent eyes.

"I…" He couldn't finish his words. He knew she spoke of the deep voiced man. He couldn't meet her innocent eyes, only subconsciously look at John's skull that stared with grim revenge at his witless murderer.

Following her brothers stare, she saw the cracked skull staring at her. Her scream was more painful than any shriek the bell could make. The Bell-ringer begged his sister to be silent. She tried to run so he held her close and begged her to be silent.

His mind was muffled by the noises. Her screams. The Bell's piercing hollow tune. John's head crumbling in his hand. His father's voice. Walter's windpipe squelching. His mother singing.

He threw his sister across the room. The thin clot which held back the pulsing blood from her earlier injury, split open.

More blood to stain the wood. She lay lifeless, her face, thankfully, turned away. The Bell-ringer heard the silent cackle of John's skull. The beast of the forest no longer lay dormant in the tree line, nor placing a single paw on the dewy grass when the night is at its darkest. No, now it lay and bathed in all its terrifying glory, in the light of day without shame.

Wandering mindlessly out into the night sky, he glanced with untold suffering at the single rose clinging on to its last crimson petal. Like a drop of thick blood.

Climbing the slippery stones to his demise, he pondered the meaning of his life. What was the point of it all if it all ends here? He knew it had to, too many had died for his life. After all, if he had been truly selfless, he would have ended his existence years ago. He thought he had to live, for his mother, to give her death purpose. But his mind that was once so clear and precise had been clouded by words of doubt. Doubt over the validity of what his father told him. Now all he wanted was to sleep.

The Bell-ringer's eyes numbly gazed upon his mother and father's grave, his dying garden and the withering rose.

"There is everything I've ever loved." He stared at the empty space around him. The town extinguished by the beast's howls. Doors locked for fear it would enter their homes. The beast needed to die. He stood ready, the cold air thawing on his pale skin. Accepting his flesh as payment. Accepting his fate. Accepting his sin. He saw what lied beneath purpose, and he planned to deliberately plummet into the void and end his torment.

The stake bore into his back. Tearing away at the flesh and scraping his spine. His life escaped in hot mist. He held on to the spire, his grip unyielding, and turned to see his sister's beautiful face. He smiled in agony, "she's alive!", he thought. One less death on his conscience. The hope of freedom from damnation, is the sweetest thing a man at the gallows can taste.

She expected a monster. A murderer. The Bell-ringer. But as if by some magical charm, she only saw a scared, handsome man look back at her, and whisper the words that would haunt her memory. Haunt her because the ghosts of her fathers' misdeeds cried with more sorrow than the ringing of a thousand bells.

"I was never here. I never existed at all". He smiled, and his grip turned loose. The last petal floated peacefully to its grave.

His last thoughts were that of a man ready for death, hoping that they could all be left. His father, mother and him, left alone to lay with each other for eternity. He thought how we are not our names, names turn silent on forgetful tongues, and fade from weak stone. We are our actions, what we do, and ultimately, we are remembered as a single entity. A priest. A whore. An uncle. A sister. A monster. That everyone will be forgotten eventually, whole lives disappearing in the inevitable oblivion, that when the sun goes cold, he was no different to anyone else. He only hoped he would be forgotten while the soil was still warm and inviting, and that he may give more life with his death than he took.

But in the winter soil. Everything is denied the merciful finality of rot.

SUPER-STATE

SUPER-STATE

A Novel of a Future Europe

BRIAN ALDISS

www.orbitbooks.co.uk

An *Orbit* Book

First published in Great Britain in 2002 by Orbit

A CIP catalogue record for this book
is available from the British Library.

ISBN 1 84149 144 6

Typeset in Bembo by Palimpsest Book Production Limited,
Polmont, Stirlingshire

Printed and bound in Great Britain by
Clays Ltd, St Ives plc

Orbit
An imprint of
Time Warner Books UK
Brettenham House
Lancaster Place
London WC2E 7EN

Some Non-Submersible Units
(we hope)
for
the ghost of
STANLEY KUBRICK
and
the living
JAN HARLAN